Pretty Birds

First in the series, Tender Heroes

Teresa Hensley

Illustrated by Cathy Cooksey

Teresa Hensley
Growing Literacy
Rocky Face, Georgia

Published by Growing Literacy
Copyright March 14, 2017

For information, please contact:
Growing Literacy
PO Box 1309
Rocky Face, GA 30740

ISBN 9781534966185

https://growingliteracy.wordpress.com/

To Nitnoie, my heroine: TH

Special thanks to my mama and sisters
for giving me the gift of story,
to my husband and children for putting up with my stories,
to Drew and Jennifer Parker for help with photography,
and my dear editors, Julie Mantooth and Libby Satterfield.

To My Uncle Charles Fettinger,

Highly decorated Vietnam Vet: CC

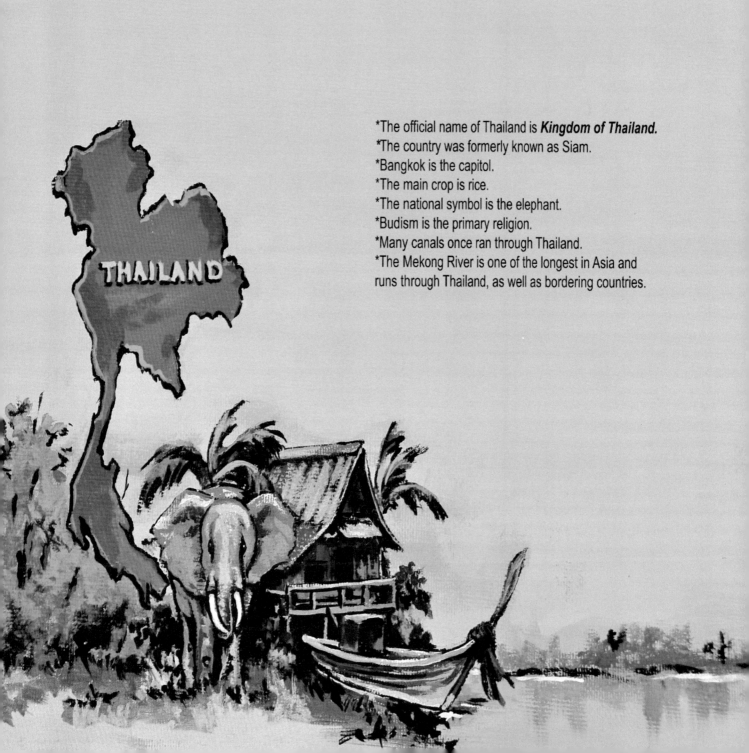

*The official name of Thailand is **Kingdom of Thailand.**
*The country was formerly known as Siam.
*Bangkok is the capitol.
*The main crop is rice.
*The national symbol is the elephant.
*Budism is the primary religion.
*Many canals once ran through Thailand.
*The Mekong River is one of the longest in Asia and runs through Thailand, as well as bordering countries.

THAILAND

Tell me again, Mama, the story in your eyes.

Behind my eyes, sweet one. The story sits right behind my eyes, where I keep my memories.

She had told her little one many times how she could close her eyes and see her homeland. Within minutes she would travel back across the water and years. Her heart would be there...on Thai soil.

Quick she would be a child again, happy one minute, sad, confused the next. She often said she tucked the story away, right behind her eyes so it would be safe.

I began collecting the pictures long ago. I needed to never forget my story.

Tell it Mama. Tell the story. Tell it all. But...sometimes when you tell it, I feel sad.

I understand sweet one. It makes me bits of sad and bits of happy, all mixed together. But it is my story. Special to me.

My favorite memory there, riding in my por's boat. Sometimes he let me go. He fished. I watched. I stood tall at the end of that long-tail boat. Brave.

Por would say, "Look child. See the river. It take you far, far from the village."

Por worried. Our village was very near a land of war. "We are too close." I heard him tell my mother many times.

Looking out at the river and up at the sky, the little girl felt small. Then, looking back toward her village, content, she felt safe in this beautiful place. Her home, her Thai home.

Por--Father

We worked rice fields, tended crops on mountain slopes. I was *noi* so I played as others worked, beside my *pee saao*. Days were hot. Long. Some days she put me on her back.

In the field we sang. I loved our work songs. I still hear one...

Pretty Bird, Pretty Bird, Sing a Pretty Song

Pretty Bird, Pretty Bird, Let me Fly with You

Nuk Soi, Nuk Soi, Throng Pang Soi.

Nuk Soi, Nuk Soi, Hih Son Bin Dop Con.

Oh, Let me Fly with You Pretty Bird
Fly Far Away with You.

Noi--Small

Pee Saao--Older Sister

She squints and places her hand on her mouth
for concentration.

This picture faded, not as clear. But I think hard and can remember. It is the
school. My brothers went. Not me. Not sister. Not other girls in the village.
Sometimes girls might go, before they were old enough to work the fields.
Just to get the numbers and the letters.

I wanted to be a boy! I wished to be a brother, not a sister. In my head I thought I may dress like
a boy, sneak inside, listen as teachers gave away the learning.

She smiled...almost. Then shook her head at the thought.

We walked halfway. Met the boys when the sun was straight up. Talk. Talk. Talk. They told
about their day.

The old school here in Palatka reminds me of that one in the village. It helps keep the
picture clear.

Her full face and round cheeks gave way to an unyielding smile. Those same lips, no doubt, had laughed when this memory was made.

Is it the elephant, Mama? The child knew which pictures brightened Mama's eyes.

Oh ELEPHANTS. Yes, Elephants!! Our village sat underneath the mountain. We did not see them a lot. Por and Mae did not like the elephants because of our crops. Be we little ones loved to see the gentle, gray giants.

If one came, my saao would try to get close. So close to count the wrinkles in his trunk. Then STOMP! His foot would thunder. She would run. Back to the field.

We would laugh and laugh at the silly girl.

Mae--Mother

Another smile...

I wish you could have seen my village. I loved it. I still love it in my memory. The way it was before.

...

Before...

She shakes her head, the picture giving way to sadness. She sees the lofty mountains, spreading across the backside of the village, like a quilt on a warm bed, it's folds offering comfort in perfect matching shades of green. Closer to the village, foilage, lush, dripping with...

...life

nd what was there, Mama?

Home. Home was there.
No homes like here. No clothes like you
have. No cars in our village. Love was
here. I was happy, safe. We played. Worked.
Lived. And the river, the river was there. I loved
t best. It sang to me. The song was loud, but peaceful.

he child waits while the river sings to her mama. She knows Mama is walking
hrough the village, visiting with people and places of long ago. She watches Mama, but doesn't
trude.

One day things began to change. Big, HUGE flying machines came to our village. I called them nuk soi. My sister and brothers laughed at me. Mae said the names of the flying machines were airplanes and helicopters.

Nuk Soi—Pretty Birds

The pretty birds, I still called them that, and the American men became part of village life. The green and gray birds brought many things to us--soap, candy, little radios, things our village did not have.

The men were our friends.

Sometimes ladies came too, not with the soldiers but friends of the soldiers. The ladies taught us how to make village life better, easier for us. Sometimes they helped if we got sick.

Then, it all felt wrong...dark, strange. The soldiers told the mothers and fathers, "Be careful. Stay alert." Mothers made children stay close. Finally, they said to find safe hiding. "Go. Quick. Quick." Sometimes we hid in big ditches the soldiers dug.

One time we had to hide in the water. I was frightened, very afraid. Mae told me, DO NOT cry. DO. NOT. MAKE. ANY. NOISE.
More and more days were like this.

Nuk soi

Nuk Soi

When your Grandpa John found me, he said I was the only sign of life in all the village...and my song, it was still alive.

And then he took you to the helicopter, right Mama?

Yes. He took me straight to the pretty bird.

He kept telling me, "Shhh. Little One.
It's okay. You're safe Little One."

I felt safe and sad all at the same time.

Looking down at the river, I felt so small and lost.

Then, the Nuk Soi took me far away from my village.

Pretty Bird, Pretty Bird, Sing a Pretty Song.
Pretty Bird, Pretty Bird, Let me Fly with You.

Oh Let Me Fly with You Pretty Bird...
--Fly Far Away with You...

The Real-life Nitnoie is now wife and mother. She came to the States
as a young child, probably about three years old. Her adopted father,
John Busby, was an American Airman for the US Airforce who
served during the Vietnam War.

Our friendship began over forty years ago, as eight-year-old girls. One tough
and full of fight, the other quiet and lost.
In a small canal community of San Mateo, Florida, we played on black sand roads
and on the banks of the canals, and I learned her story there
--survivor of war.
I watched her. I learned from her how to fight demons,
stay strong, and love hard.

Love to you my friend,
my tender hero.

Facts & Stats:

- 1954-1975 The war lasted a little over 20 years.
- The soils of South Vietnam, North Vietnam, Cambodia, and Laos all saw military conflict.
- The United States' involvement was from 1961 to 1975.
- The USAF was positioned in Thailand during the war.
- Eighty percent of airstrikes on North Vietnam originated out of Thailand.
- US troops involved were 8,744,000.
- US battle deaths were approximately 47,410.
- Total estimated causalities for the entire war, including civilian were 1,313,000.
- The assassination of US President, John F. Kennedy happened during the United States' involvement in the war.
- The United States withdrew from the war.
- After the war, Indonesia, Singapore, Thailand, Malaysia, and the Philippines declared solidarity against communist expansion.
- Thailand and the US were allies.
- US Airforce flew strikes on Vietnam out of Thailand.

Teresa Hensley has worked in public education for eighteen years. She is a literacy/instructional coach by day and a writer by night. She and her husband of thirty-two years live in a small community in North Georgia. Together they have three grown children, their mates, and one grandson. Teresa's passions are Christ, family, gardening, writing, and literacy education. She enjoys working with teachers and students; she has led many courses on literacy, as well as presented at national literacy conferences. *Pretty Birds* is her first published work.

https://growingliteracy.wordpress.com

Cathy Cooksey is a self-taught artist who paints primarily with acrylics, but also enjoys pencil. She loves to paint historical subjects and has over sixty prints of her paintings. Her work has been shown in the US Capitol, the Georgia State Capitol, several museums, as well as having current displays in public and government venues. Cathy is a wife, mother of three, and grandmother. She is a 911 operator and lives in Ringgold, Ga. Her illustrations have appeared in four published books.

https://www.etsy.com/shop/Brushedmemories
https://www.facebook.com/Brushedmemories

Made in the USA
San Bernardino, CA
07 April 2018